# Brave Little Spot

by **Della Rowland**

**illustrated by Loretta Lustig**

**GT**
PUBLISHING
NEW YORK

Little Spot lived in Firehouse Number 6 with her mother and father.
They were Dalmatians, the official firehouse dog, and they were more
than just pets. They were part of the Number 6 Firefighting Team!

Little Spot's mother and father wore special badges on their collars with their names on them. Little Spot couldn't wait until she was big enough to have a badge of her own.

Little Spot's family came from a long line of brave firehouse dogs. "Once we were called coach dogs," her mother told her. "Back in the days before cars, horses pulled the fire engines. The coach dogs ran ahead to clear the way for the horses."

"Now we help the firefighters every way we can, dear.
And when you're a little bit bigger, you'll join us."

It was late on a stormy night when the alarm sounded. Little Spot's mother and father hurried to their places in the truck. The sleepy firefighters pulled on their high black boots and long yellow slickers. No one noticed Little Spot hiding in the hose.

Little Spot thought she was already big enough to help out at a fire. But nobody else did. Each time the fire trucks rolled out of the firehouse, she was left behind.

But one night, Little Spot finally had her chance.

The fire truck zoomed out of the firehouse with the siren blaring. It turned a corner so fast that Little Spot rolled out of the hose—and right into a firefighter. "You shouldn't be here, Little Spot," he told her firmly.

But it didn't matter. It was too late to take Little Spot back to the firehouse.

The fire truck pulled up to a burning house. Smoke was pouring out of the windows, and the flames made loud crackling noises. Little Spot trembled. "Now you stay back, Little Spot," her father barked sternly.

A little girl ran to her father's side. "One of the kittens is still in the basement," she sobbed.

"I'm sorry, honey," said her father. "But the fire chief said it was too dangerous to go inside."

"I'll rescue the kitten!" thought Little Spot. And before anyone could stop her, she ran straight for the basement door.

The basement was full of thick smoke that stung Little Spot's eyes and made her cough. "I didn't know it would be so hard to breathe in a fire," she thought. "And how will I find the kitten if I can't see?"

Just then she heard mewing. She pricked up her ears and followed the sound. Little Spot didn't even see the kitten until she bumped right into it! *Meoww!* The frightened kitten swatted her on the nose!

"*Ooww!*" yelped Little Spot. "I was just trying to help you!"

Little Spot grabbed the kitten by the scruff of its neck and began crawling back to the stairs. Suddenly, the ceiling collapsed and came crashing down around her! She ducked her head and tried to dodge the falling beams but the fire scorched her coat. Several times she almost dropped the kitten when a hot ember burned her nose.

Everywhere she turned there were hot orange flames. "I'll never find my way out!" she howled.
Then . . . she saw a thin beam of light shining down through the smoke.

"A flashlight!" she thought happily. "The firefighters are shining a flashlight down here so they can find me!" She followed the beam until she bumped into a wall. No, it wasn't a wall. It was the staircase! Now she could get out!

But the top of the stairs seemed so far away. As she scrambled up the first step, she wondered if she would make it.

Suddenly, strong arms scooped up Little Spot and the kitten. She felt herself being carried away from the hot smoky building to where the air was cool and clear. Hands took the kitten from her mouth and Little Spot began to pant.

Little Spot opened her eyes to cheering. To her surprise, everyone was looking at her!

"You made it, Little Spot!" exclaimed her mother.

"And you rescued the kitten!" her father barked proudly.

"You're a hero!" cried the little girl, throwing her arms around Little Spot.

The next morning the firefighters at Firehouse Number 6 put a new
collar on Little Spot. It was a grown-up dog's collar. Hanging from it
was her very own shiny badge.

The name on the badge read BIG SPOT.

"You were pretty brave out there last night," said a firefighter.
"Looks like you're part of the Number 6 Firefighting Team now."

Little Spot's mother and father beamed proudly at her side.